XENO RECKONING

by Paul Heingarten

Published by Decatur Media
New Orleans, Louisiana
www.decaturmedia.com

ISBN: # 978-0-9972626-8-1

Cover design by Y. Nikolova at Ammonia Book Covers

<u>Acknowledgements</u>

First and foremost, thank you to my wife Andrea, thank you for loving me and for your endless support, I couldn't do this without you.

To my family, for endless love, support, and encouragement.

To Lisa Herrington, thank you once again for your friendship and pep talks!

To Jenny Bodle, I'm so glad we met. You've gone beyond being a PA and I consider you a good friend. Looking forward to collaborating with you in the future.

To Carissa Andrews, for being such a beacon of positivity and support, and for taking time to interact with me amid my endless series of questions.

To the Bayou Writers Club. Thank you for hours of discussions about writing, the camaraderie, and for your support.

Special thanks to my street team, the "Krewe of Paul" for helping me become the best writer I can. Find out about the Krewe of Paul and get free books at my site www.paulheingarten.com

For Andrea, with all my love

Chapter 1

SELINA RAVENCRAFT LOOKED OUT THE WINDOW at an arriving transport. It was mid-morning, but even the twin suns of the Zormad system hadn't managed to break through the clouds yet. On the nearby landing pad stood a collection of people waiting to be loaded aboard the arriving ship.

Selina lived with several thousand humans, refugees from Earth living on a colony on Zormad called NewEarth. She watched the groups of ten each, lined up and chained together on the landing pad outside. She wondered how much they second guessed what they did wrong or just what they messed up that had gotten them caught. These offenders were called Lookers because of their specific offense of crossing over dimensions, also known as Dimencrime. Lookers used their unique ability to commit Dimencrime involving theft, vandalism, and in some cases, murder. Selina hadn't any idea how Lookers came to do what they did, but regardless, she was part of the Regulation, an agency tasked with keeping order.

While in the past, 'order' meant a steady hand over the citizens of NewEarth and Zormad in general, more recently the issue of Lookers had become a prominent concern for all interested in upholding the peace, fragile as it was.

Selina hopped in her bio sanitizing unit to get ready for the day. Stepping out a few moments later, she slipped into her uniform and munched on some breakfast rations before she headed down to her Precinct.

Earth had become untenable for some time, and a group of brighter minds had had the foresight and ability to focus energy on an evacuation. The response from many wasn't unlike what a certain Noah had gotten many centuries earlier, but once again, preparation and perception won out over disbelief.

A series of probes had pointed the human exodus mission to Zormad. With a climate close enough to Earth to be livable and a token offering of provisions to a world recovering from a great famine, the last of the human race were given a chance to start again on a system neither made for nor particularly happy with their presence.

Formerly a bustling system of industry, Zormad reeled from its most recent famine that left the choice of survival to those willing to do whatever to hoard the meager resources still left.

NewEarth consisted of a Network of cobbled together buildings, most of them constructed from the remnants of the former Ark Ship that humans traveled in to Zormad. The enormous craft languished in a state of progressive disassembly, its pieces gradually removed and arranged in

Spartanesque towns of buildings with a definitive refugee motif in construction. The power reactor from the ship was also repurposed for town energy uses, and an agricultural area designated for crop production.

As awful as Zormad was for being a good or even decent destination for the last of Earth's human race, the original settlers of NewEarth remembered enough of their former home to know that even Zormad was a step ahead of the place they left behind.

Humans' ability to somehow cultivate rudimentary crops in the Zormad soil gave them the basest of acceptance on a system still in a pandemic of want.

Within twenty years on Zormad, humans' positions grew a little, and their initial baby steps on their adopted home grew in stride, where basic crop production continued on a small scale.

Chapter 2

SELINA HEADED INTO THE REGULATION OFFICE but first stopped at the hydration port for a fill up of precious H20. One of the larger issues that remained for NewEarth, the arid land of Zormad left them scraping by for the aquatic sustenance they had in plenty on Earth. Selina was glad for her share from the Regulation office, which she gladly took away from the eyes of other NewEarth residents who still adjusted to the lower amount of water available overall.

Jared, her shift lieutenant, greeted Selina once she arrived. His burly frame slouched as he studied his hand-held digital readout screen of the latest report of Looker sightings. Among the sightings and crimes, a name surfaced over and over again: Malone. There wasn't so much as a face to go with the name, but he hadn't needed even that for the reputation he commanded.

"Morning, sir," Selina muttered as she leaned in a bit to Jared.

Jared's eyes met hers. "That it is. Care to explain this business from your last shift, Officer Ravencraft?"

There it was. Her breakfast had barely started digesting, and Selina was given her first serving of crap for the day. The good Lieutenant referred to the sighting Selina worked where a Looker appeared with a set of stolen artifacts and vanished, but not before making off with her weapon as well.

Selina felt the back of her neck go cold. She'd been on a routine run about the market in the NewEarth colony. She remembered the hairs on her arm stood on end and a strange sound, like the fluttering of insect wings, and before she realized it, she was knocked to the ground, and her gun was yanked from her grasp. She got a look at the thief, a bluish glowing figure with long hair and a beard. He gave her a smirk before he pummeled her gut and vanished, leaving her with no weapon and even less of an explanation for her shift supervisor. "It's not like I handed it to him, ya know. He snuck me with a tase and laid me out before I could get a handle on 'em."

Jared's mouth drew in a line. "Excuses, Ravencraft. Losing weaponry is bad enough, but when you're up against a Looker, you gotta be more careful than that. I know you're new here; how long has it been?"

"Six weeks." Selina was amazed when she realized she'd already been with the Regulation that long. It seemed like she had joined the ranks yesterday. A lot of people had encouraged it, especially her mother. Even though her father Erick wasn't around, Selina knew he would've been for it as well, as much as he'd done for NewEarth. Erick had a lot to do with setting up NewEarth's initial structure and government. He was in the first group of humans to set foot on Zormad. While they were the legacy bearers of that blue-green ball of life humans had called home for centuries, Earth soon became the talk of stories on its journey into becoming more of a fairy tale than a physical world. For the subsequent generations of humans on Zormad, Earth became little more than a series of legends, lessons carried over from a world forgotten by necessity, abandoned by requirement. The early colony of NewEarth took a lot of effort and diplomacy, first in managing to secure a location in the Zormad wilderness and to make contact with the locals and establish a presence. Through a combination of a little effort and much more persistence and stubbornness, humans forged a fragile but establishing presence on their new home.

Erick helped establish the Regulation, and even helped humans make inroads with their neighbors on Zormad. Selina figured it was her turn to chip in and make sure she did what her father would've wanted her to do. However, being daughter to someone like Erick also involved an eternal stay within a shadow of accomplishment, and Selina dreaded the day she was measured up to what dear old dad pulled off in his life, even though his was cut short when he was killed in a raid of NewEarth by Railen.

Jared offered a smile and patted her shoulder. He didn't have to be a clairvoyant to know Selina's history, and he always admired her resolve. "OK, Selina. Six weeks is still kinda green. But you've gotta understand, losing a weapon is serious. We have enough problems now without more tech getting into the hands of Lookers."

"I know, I know. There's just so much to keep track of, with the Railen and the Omegans milling around." Selina shrugged.

Jared nodded. "Yeah, the Railen and Omegan fight has gone on way longer than our being here, but there's a good chance we'll catch some of that action too." He smiled. "I thought you had a lot of promise, giving who your dad was and all, and you were one of the best out of Training we'd seen in a while. Maybe, though, we rushed getting you out there solo."

"I made the cut, Jared, top level on marksmanship and tactics, and even your best boys couldn't dust me on the track." Even saying the word, Selina thought about how silly it was. The 'track' for NewEarth was essentially the perimeter of the colony, a decent 10 miles in distance, but long enough that all of the Regulation got more than a healthy workout running it.

"Selina, you got the fundamentals down, no doubt. But this job's about more than checking off a PT list. Our work's 98% instinct, and that doesn't come with a quick course time. There's plenty to throw down on out there. You need to have a solid grasp of the world we're in now. Trust me, there's any number of people, especially the Mardak, who'd love to blame any old problem they have on us. Remember, we're the outsiders. Any problem that gets pinned on us is way harder to disprove." Jared chewed his lip. His eyes spun off in thought for a moment before a glimmer popped and he gave Selina a smile. "I know what."

As new as Selina was, she already knew when Jared or any of her superiors flashed the look like Jared's face showed right then, it was from an idea, and any of these were things she never enjoyed much, if at all.

"You're getting a partner. I'm setting you up with Wexan."

Selina felt her gut tighten and the roots of indigestion taking hold. "Really. You're gonna put me with one of them... now?"

Jared squared his shoulders. "Wexan's a decorated vet with over fifteen years steady service."

"He's also a Mardak." Selina folded her arms.

The Mardak were the primary race of Zormad when humans established NewEarth on the system two decades earlier. In that time humans managed a more or less fragile peace with the Mardak and other visiting beings. However, with the issue of the Lookers on the rise, and Railen and Omegan's posturing nearing lethal levels, tensions flared more each passing day.

The sentient races on Zormad like the Mardaks had, through decades of a lifestyle of plenty, grown more accustomed to an existence of receiving than of creating and giving when it came to the basics for survival. The famine left the more adaptable with the choice of what they were willing to do to live until the next week and beyond.

"Selina, I don't care what you think or believe about Mardaks. We've got way bigger problems to worry about."

Selina swallowed hard. She knew what Jared meant. In addition to the Lookers, and the turf war the Railen and Omegans seemed hellbent on, there was also a strange virus that had been rampant in the Galaxy. The contacts NewEarth made with the Mardaks on Zormad referred to it as "Veculus". They weren't exactly sure how it was transmitted, but humans were given plenty of warning and threats by the Mardaks, enough that gave humans the idea Mardaks considered them to blame for the strange illness.

Jared glanced up at a screen on the wall that displayed counts of NewEarth residents. It was both a status update and a goal, the silent hope of all in the Regulation that the number of

NewEarth only increased over time. "It's not the time to be relaxed. The Mardaks aren't exactly thrilled we're here to begin with."

"What's that word they use for us?"

"Xeno. And you best get used to that, 'cause that's what everyone thinks of us. Dirty, stinky Xeno, who infected Ling Galaxy. Even with the regular shipments of crops we're sending to Tas Ralong and other towns, Mardak are dying to use any reason to remove us, up to and including blaming crimes and Veculus on us. We've gotta make a show of good faith to them that we're on their side working these problems in earnest."

Selina shrugged. "Yes, sir."

Chapter 3

TAS RALONG JUT OUT OF THE POWDERY DRY land just to the east of NewEarth. Its wide array of streets snaked around large collections of buildings that thrust from the sandy floor like appendages of someone buried alive. While some structures soared several hundred feet into the air, others were humbler in appearance.

Once a prominent center of industry, Tas Ralong and its wide collection of denizens had since been well on a collective journey down the path toward oblivion. That trip lingered along enough so the devious had plenty of chances for swindles and cons before all life was truly sucked from the land. Tas Ralong was also a good place to go if you wanted to hide, provided you weren't out for trouble you weren't able to handle. A large number of smugglers and soldiers for hire found its somewhat loose concern for the law a nice amenity, similar to several other outlying systems in Ling Galaxy. Syndicates, groups of smugglers organized into even more disreputable fronts of villainy, hung their banners freely, especially on the Trading Markets that provided the closest thing to a sustainable economy Zormad had seen in many years. To the outsider, Tas Ralong had a feel of a great metropolis that had missed the memo about its obsolescence long ago.

The towering buildings still offered a good amount of occupancy, but the industry that once powered the town had mostly gone away, leaving a once proud but now crumbled infrastructure, where the economy of greed and the industry of the quick and questionable trading markets ruled supreme.

The Regulation of NewEarth had begun a cooperation with the Mardak Sentries. The Regulation assisted the Mardak patrols of Tas Ralong in exchange for a slightly better attitude by the Mardaks about several thousand putrid earthlings chewing up miles of real estate on Zormad. Together with the crop sharing gesture, it moved the needle on the Mardak attitude about humans a hair more toward the tolerance side, for some Mardaks anyway. As a slight gesture in response, the Mardaks forced the Sentries who were paired with officers of the Regulation to learn basic English, which did two things: it created a group of Mardaks who spoke choppy and broken English, and it gave certain Mardaks even more reason to hate humans.

Selina and Wexan's introduction was handled without much pomp at all. She hated the quickness she was handed off to this assignment, and from Wexan's surly glance, she figured the feeling was mutual. They faced each other outside the Mardak Sentry post near a line of street patrol craft.

Wexan took his time notating things on his personal tablet device, then looked back at Selina. "What are you, ten years old?"

"I'm 25, dude. Nice shape you're in. Guess you don't miss many meals, including other people's?"

Wexan grunted with a glare. "Listen, Xeno. In NewEarth you do anything your little Xeno mind wants. Here in Tas Ralong, you do what I say. I got enough to worry about without a Xeno messing things up."

Selina swallowed and shook her head slightly. The sooner her shift ended, the better.

Wexan nodded toward a hover patrol vehicle. "Let's go."

The next fifteen minutes of their shift went down mostly in silence. Neither was crazy about breaking the void with conversation, when the only starters that came to mind were things like "How soon can your kind get the hell off my system?" or "Why do Mardaks smell that bad; is it genetic or do you have to work at it?"

As a distraction from chatting, Selina checked the HUD in her helmet. The Regulation wore special digivisors that provided real time info on all creatures that came into view. Another aspect of the agreement with the Mardak allowed the HUD in Regulation gear to be loaded with the latest Mardak data on criminal activity.

Passersby on the paths near the street were identified on sight, and if the individual had any warrants, a reddish block appeared next to them along with an alert message to the wearer of the Digivisor. It was then up to them to figure out the best way to apprehend the person, how much force was necessary, and how much of a risk was involved.

Once she'd exhausted all reasonable excuses for ignoring her new partner, Selina decided work was the best topic. She looked at the Mardaks and other beings who walked on the street while her HUD cascaded updates on each that passed across her viewpane. "So, heard about any criminals here these days?"

Wexan snorted and coughed. For a second Selina, wondered if that was going to be his only contribution, but he soon found
his gravelly voice. "Utility theft's the big problem. Stealing converters, energy supplies. Really putting a strain on what's left here."

"Any idea who's involved?" Selina asked. "What about the Syndicates?"

"No, that's too small for them. They're into Essence and bigger prizes like bulk vehicle hauls, UA Credit theft."

Selina nodded. The most widely accepted currency in Ling Galaxy, UA Credits were guaranteed on all worlds within the Universal Alliance and therefore were one of the preferred currencies of the criminal minded. This was especially the case on Zormad, where basic citizens were only concerned with their own survival. Groups like the Syndicates dealt in UA Credits at the trading markets that held space in every major town on the system.

"What about Dimencrime; seen any in Tas Ralong lately?"

Wexan threw Selina a perturbed look. "You kidding? In just the last two years, they've gone from two or three cases in a month to four or five a week."

The problems with Lookers began with things as innocent as simple theft and public spectacles, as much as any theft was innocent, anyway. Jumping across dimensions allowed

Lookers to bounce between locations hundreds or even thousands of miles away. Items like energy generation tech and weapons gave them plenty of theft options for sport, but the black markets sometimes requested more specific services, which brought on several cases of kidnappings and a slew of murders.

It was on the tip of Selina's tongue to talk about her own run-in with Dimencrime and the Looker, but she held quiet. The last thing she needed on her first shift with a Mardak was even more doubt of her worth.

When they stopped for cross traffic, Wexan sighed. "The hunt for Essence has never been stronger. At least the Nara were nice and careful to keep Essence hidden, or we'd be in for way more problems."

The only thing that could've possibly made life on Zormad worse than their current existence was the absence of Essence. The substance resided on Zormad, and every world in Ling Galaxy, as a source for life on its system. Essence was deposited on each world by the Nara since the dawn of Ling Galaxy as the life sustaining force and replenished periodically. The lack of Essence on a world meant its sure destruction.

Selina noticed an open field to the right of their path. The area was littered with a series of tents, and she knew by the way they were set up that it was a temp hospital for housing Veculus patients.

"What about Veculus then?" Selina muttered.

"You tell me, Xeno. I thought your kind buggered us all up with that junk."

Selina shot Wexan a glare. "Think again, dude. You know that crud was here way before us."

Many other worlds in Ling Galaxy had a better lot than Zormad and her fellow downtrodden, and had managed a life of moderate to greater happiness. But worlds of drought and lack like Zormad left many of her residents wondering about the Essence and the true nature of the Nara, and just how this source of life of all worlds existed, while so much suffering did too. Furthermore, others believed the existence of Essence and its usage were handled wrong, and sometimes redistribution was necessary to allow those who had less to at least know a life without hunger.

"You ever seen it? The Essence?" asked Selina.

Wexan scoffed. "Nobody getting near Essence and living to tell about it, unless they're a Nara. Remember that good, Xeno."

While Essence was kept on each world, finding it was nowhere near as simple as canvassing the system. The Nara constructed a repository on each world for holding the Essence orb necessary to sustain life and keep that world intact.
Locating this portal required the ability to shift dimensions, which made Lookers not only a threat to the lawful, but a tool for the nefarious.

Wexan swung their vehicle up a tight curve around an abandoned warehouse. "We don't need to worry about Essence. Besides, there's enough Energy Tech theft to worry about. How about we make ourselves useful, keep an eye on the markets, see where that stuff's turning up."

"You mean the ones outside of town?"

"Mmmhmmm." Wexan cast a slanted grin toward her. "You sound nervous. Think you can handle the rough types?"

Selina wasn't about to let anyone push her, especially a Mardak. "I'm up for whatever you are; just get us there."

Wexan chuckled. "Now you're talking. So, Xeno, tell me about yourself."

"Why do you wanna know?" Selina's midsection tightened. Wexan's sudden probe felt more like an interrogation than just co-worker chit chat.

Wexan's eyes narrowed. "Because we're partners. And one of us may have to save the other's ass. If that should happen and it's me, the more I know about your sorry Xeno self, the more likely I'll give a damn about saving you."

Selina shook her head and wondered how anyone from Earth ever got the bright idea humans would ever be accepted in a place like Zormad. "I was born after the relocation. About twenty years ago. My mom raised me. My dad, he wasn't around."

"What happened to him?"

"The Railen killed him." Selina's throat tightened with her answer. It was as much as she wanted to share with a Mardak for the moment, but truthfully it wasn't too far from everything she knew about her father's death. Like her fellow NewEarth residents, Selina had no idea about the conflict between the Railen and Omegans, other than it occasionally involved a close call for humans by one or the other. Selina knew both races were on a rampage to control Ling Galaxy, and on one occasion NewEarth found itself in the path of a Railen raid of NewEarth. Selina's father had led a group that held their own, though it later proved costly when the Railen returned for revenge. The reminder of that still stung, it always would.

"Is that right?" Wexan's gaze lingered on Selina for a moment, then he eased their vehicle on further through the streets of Tas Ralong.

Selina knew for her own sake anything she said, even if it was nothing at all, was better than verbal trips down her family history with anyone, especially a Mardak.

Selina had begun a mental note of exactly how many minutes were left into their shift when the vehicle console sounded an alert. "Incendiary charge activated."

Wexan grunted. "Where? Get location."

"Scanning. Quadrant 87, approximate distance, 2.7 miles, ETA less than five minutes."

Wexan slammed the shift lever down. The engine at the front of their vehicle roared angrily as they shot ahead.

Selina readied her pulse rifle. "Probably Railen; they've been rousing the Omegans lately."

"Maybe so. I'm gonna activate the tase net; see if we can pull them in for intel."

Selina shrugged. If it was Railen, she figured attempts at intel were as useless as painting a building with one fingernail.

A few quick turns and there they saw the scene. A former industrial district, the far end of the street wrapped into a cul-de-sac bordered by a collection of high-rise buildings. Several disabled vehicles were scattered around the center of the streets. Behind them were two squads, one Railen and one Omegan, each of which held opposing sides of the street in an active skirmish. Blasts tore through the tall buildings on the side of the street and sent shards of steel and stone through the air along with wafts of dust that hung over the scene like tattered drapery.

Selina ran a cursory scan with her Digivisor. The readout relayed a series of scans of the rubble scattered about the area as well as an assessment of the two groups engaged in a firefight of sporadic pulse weapon fire. Most important, Selina's HUD confirmed several building occupants aside from the brawling groups ahead of them.

"We've got bystanders in at least one building ahead," Selina muttered.

Wexan eyed the scene for a minute while he munched his lip. "This is more than a simple extraction. We're letting the militia handle this."

The ground shook with a blast. Selina ducked low out of instinct. "The militia? What week are they getting here? That fight just broke out. Those buildings have people in them; we have to clear anyone we can to safety!"

Wexan grabbed a handful of Selina's shirt and yanked her close. "Listen, rookie. You go out there, only thing you're gonna clear is a few pulse blasts into your body. Stay your ass here, I'm not filling out a lot of reports because you wanted to be a hero. This is a turf war; it happens all the time."

Selina eyed Wexan in disbelief.

Wexan narrowed his eyes and continued. "Think you're the only one who lost somebody here? We've lived with this for a long time, understand? Just like we've put up with Veculus, and even you Xeno. In fact, we dealt with these brawls way before Xeno ever came here. Railen and Omegans are trying to see who can grab more land. I can't tell you how many of these I've seen in all my years of service. The Mardak Militia's way better armed for this, and you oughta know that."

Selina grit her teeth. She picked up a pair of heat signals on the ground and sure enough, zoomed her viewfinder on two

Mardaks huddled behind a transit station thirty yards ahead. She sucked in a deep breath and activated her armor. The nano metallic fibers wove themselves around her body in an instant, quickly fastened and became an airtight suit that included her visor. As she tapped the door release and leaped to the street, Wexan bellowed, "Get back here!"

Selina hopped before she shot Wexan a glare. "Sorry, but I'm not here to sit on my ass. Circle back the way we came; I'll grab those stranded Mardaks out there."

"Get back here, now," Wexan growled.

Selina smirked and cast another glance toward the fray before her eyes met Wexan's most disapproving glare. "Double back; meet you when I grab them."

Wexan barked something in Mardak that Selina knew wasn't a term of affection toward her. She grinned and darted towards the transit station. Her visor readout indicated the thermal detonation was imminent, based on the intensity of the signature.

Another blast shook the ground and knocked Selina on her belly. She looked ahead and saw she was just a few feet from the station, so she scrambled up and slid under the small roof to

find two Mardaks. They were clearly dressed like lab workers of some kind.

Selina activated her in-set translator so she spoke to them in Mardak and heard them in English. The Mardaks flinched at the sight of her but relaxed a bit when they noticed her Regulation uniform. "Hi there; want a ride?"

One of the Mardaks, heavyset with stringy gray hair, replied, "Yes, please, help us!"

Selina jabbed a finger back up the street. "My partner is that way. Head there, take a left at that first corner, and look for a Tas Ralong Sentry vehicle. I'll follow behind."

Not surprisingly, the two Mardaks needed no convincing and took off in a half quick trot. Selina crouched low as she jogged. A pulse shot seared the building slightly ahead of where the Mardaks ran, and Selina got off a few return volleys of her own back toward the fray behind them.

They were almost to the corner when Selina's display sent another message. "Detonator activated, shelter in place."

The blast knocked Selina to the ground and sent a cascade of rubble down the street in their direction. She strained her eyes through the haze until she saw the Mardaks. They were on their feet but gazed back at her confusedly.

"Keep going!" Selina bellowed. As she got to her feet, the dull thuds of pulse fire slamming into the ground sounded behind her. She looked and saw three of the Omegan squad had, for whatever reason, decided Selina was as good a target as anything. Maybe her rescuees were more than innocent bystanders after all.

She was fifty feet from the corner, and when the Mardaks disappeared behind it, she juked on her path, avoiding the weapon fire that spread from one end of the street to the other. The barrage ripped into buildings but also portions of the roadway a little too close to Selina for her liking. "Wexan, need help asap, taking fire."

Selina rolled to the ground behind a disabled vehicle and looked up. The three Omegans were on foot about twenty feet away. Their reptilian faces twisted in snarls, their reddish eyes shot back a cold and heartless look toward her. She felt the Omegans weren't so much living beings as they were some kind of drones, commanded and set loose on the world like an infection. The Railen weren't much better, but it seemed they had some sense of reason in their heads, even though that reason was pretty twisted in itself.

Selina activated her rifle and returned fire from behind her cover position. Her shots made contact on one of the Omegans, but it glanced off the armor, and aside from some stray sparks, they responded with guttural snarls of defiance.

The power store on her weapon was low, but she remembered from her training about the incendiary setting on standard weapons. It exhausted the power store in a few quick blasts, but if you were in a back against the wall kind of situation, it was a handy option. Several shots from the Omegans punched into the busted vehicle and knocked her back a few feet. She activated the incendiary round and slid from behind her cover. She quickly got to a standing position and charged, her weapon aloft, and a stream of brilliant white beams shot toward the Omegans. The nearest one was sliced in two from the shot; the others kept their fire up but were silenced when the remaining rounds found their mark.

Selina skid to a halt and tried catching her breath. She'd just looked at her handiwork when her HUD registered another alert, but Selina saw what it was without help from her tech.

"Wexan, the Omegans have a hovercraft; move your ass or I'm toast!" Selina hollered.

A few seconds later, she heard the familiar rumble of their vehicle. Once Selina dashed back and jumped in, Wexan pulled away.

Their sentry vehicle careened back down the streets of Tas Ralong as a Militia Vehicle roared past them down the street for the rest of the mop up. As Selina connected her spent weapon up to the recharge console, Wexan activated the privacy screen between them and their passengers.

"What the hell was that back there?"

"I dunno, your usual skirmish between the—"

"Not the fight. You and that hero stunt?" Wexan glared.

Selina felt a lump in her throat. Her years growing up without a father had taken their toll on her but also fostered a fierce sense of action. Her joining the Regulation felt right to Selina at the time. She never thought long enough where her drive came from, but she figured at least part of her attitude was wanting to show she was like her father: proud, determined, maybe a bit stubborn. In a deeper part of her mind lay the wonder if the reason she kept so active was coping over the pain of her father's loss, something she never addressed but had only endured so far. In any case, to Wexan, someone she'd barely known, she knew instinctively he neither needed nor deserved a full brief of her reasons, especially when she wasn't even sure of them herself.

"It's called saving lives, Wexan. See these two behind us? If I hadn't grabbed them, they'd have been vaporized by the time the militia arrived."

Wexan jabbed a shaky finger into Selina's face. "You don't know who we saved; they coulda been the ones who started that mess. Hell, they coulda been trying to find Essence. Your little sortie was damned risky. Militia's got platoons of boots for these kinds of fights. They take the big threats, the invasions, things like that. We handle small stuff, petty thefts, maybe smugglers if they aren't too big a threat. You best keep that in mind if you want to live much longer."

Selina shrugged him off. She figured on one hand he had a point; that fight could've easily ended bad for her pretty quick. The pulse rifles they carried were for pacification mostly, not military grade tech for extended engagements. But something else in her knew there was no way she'd have let those Mardaks go without helping them. As much as Mardaks and humans hadn't completely gotten over their tensions, she still felt like they at least owed Mardaks for the chance to start NewEarth, and without more efforts at working together, neither race survived in the end with all they faced.

They returned to the Tas Ralong Sentry precinct, where their next requirement was handing the Mardaks back for safe return to their residence once the militia returned an all clear for the area where the fight took place.

Wexan and Selina escorted the Mardaks to the holding area for refugees. As they walked over, Selina caught a glimpse of one of them, the shorter heavyset one, as they looked back at her with a bit of wonder. She just figured the sight of a human was a little uncommon for them.

But still, as they walked, she felt the Mardak's gaze still on her to the point she became uncomfortable. Selina stopped; her eyes locked on the Mardak.

Wexan, after a few steps, also noticed Selina's stare off. "Move!" Wexan barked.

Selina's eyes were fixed on the Mardak. "Gimme a minute, Wexan; I'm getting a vibe here."

Wexan padded up, a lingering growl under his breath as he slowly shouldered his rifle. Selina activated her translator again and peered into the Mardak's eyes. "Is something wrong?"

The Mardak chuckled a bit. "Pardon me, I don't mean to stare. We Mardaks have a tendency to study new people we've met, as our belief is in this grand universe we're all connected in some way. Pardon my rudeness, my name is Grisha Eld."

"Selina Ravencraft."

Grisha smiled warmly. "Suddenly a name makes one less ominous, no?"

Selina's lips curved up slightly. "I guess."

"You're the first Xeno I've met. I understand your kind came from a distant galaxy."

"Yep. And we didn't bring Veculus if that's what you're thinking."

Grisha chuckled. "Oh, I'd suspect the Railen or Omegans of Veculus before the likes of a Xeno."

Selina nodded. "We're just trying to make our way and help where we can."

"As are we all. In any case, Selina Ravencraft, the truth of the matter is you and my brother Mardak over there risked your lives for mine today, and as such I feel obliged to show you some act of kindness."

With that, Grisha pulled at his cloak for a moment. "I've found something that you might deem useful. I believe the Omegans were looking for it when they attacked the Railen back where you found us." With that he produced a slender device. The sliver outer coat of the item gleamed, even in the moderate light of the depot. It was shaped like a pistol with a greenish display at one end. He offered it to Selina.

The device felt cool in her hand. She held it up and examined it in the light. Wexan noticed her with the item and blurted, "How the hell did you get that?"

Grisha's eyes darted between Wexan and Selina, but he only managed a grunt in response. Wexan grabbed Grisha by his cloak and lifted him up. Grisha's eyes widened, and he let loose with a surprised whimper. Unfazed, Wexan leaned in. "That thing's contraband if it's what I think it is, so start talking."

"It was dropped by a Railen. I swear, I'd never seen it before!" Grisha protested.

Selina held the item up. It could've been a pulse pistol, for what she knew. She felt a trigger where one typically would be. She held it overhead, pointed in a firing position and her finger slid toward the trigger.

She heard Wexan's warning, "Selina, better put that down!" but before she knew what else, a shock rocketed through her body and knocked her unconscious.

Chapter 4

SELINA WOKE IN THE MARDAK INFIRMARY. Monitors beeped around her, and the room opened into a larger area filled with the bustle of medics working on the sick. Wexan sat beside her bed but was on his feet soon after her eyes opened. "You're just determined to get yourself in trouble, aren't ya?"

"You're not gonna start acting like you care now, are you, Wexan?" Selina's attempt at a laugh quickly dissolved in a painful coughing fit. She grunted and tried moving herself up in bed. Her efforts at sitting up rewarded her with a piercing headache that bored through the center of her skull, and she lay back in a series of groans.

Wexan eyed Selina with a gaze she hadn't seen from him yet. She'd have sworn his eyes had a stain of compassion on them.

"Look, just because you're a Xeno and all... damn it, I'm responsible for anyone on my watch." Wexan coughed a bit before he blinked and glanced away for a moment.

Selina focused her breaths, hoping it calmed her aches. "What happened? Last thing I remember was—"

"Ignoring what I said about putting that device down. Maybe next time you'll listen. Well, our little friend we picked up was more than just a refugee. I had a feeling on that tech so I ran it, and sure enough. It's a Railen Tracker. They use them for locating Lookers."

Selina's eyes widened. "I didn't even know that was possible."

"It is, and whoever gets a hold of one has a huge advantage trying to find Essence."

"So, the Railen are tracking them?"

"The Railen are, plus anyone else with half a brain. First thing I thought seeing those two squads fighting was it was just another rumble between Omegans and Railen, you know, regular stuff. But this tracker, with these around now, it tells me they've got good reason to think Lookers are here. They can't catch a Looker without one of these. The tracker not only locates but incapacitates the Lookers and any other moron who doesn't know how to disengage the safety mechanism."

Selina rubbed her head and hoped the throbbing stopped soon. "Where's the tracker now?"

"Got it on me. I was gonna turn it into Central Security, but I thought better we hang onto it, and see what we can find out at the Trading Markets."

"Sounds good to me. How about the Omegans? They didn't look exactly happy to see us back there."

"Omegans are pissed from centuries of being someone else's errand boy. Former protectors of the Nara, the Omegans invested lots of time in their service and are ready to build their own empire. They've finally got it in their heads that in the grand scheme of things every race has their time to ascend to the top of the order and their turn is now. They've been getting bolder and bolder, and the Railen are one of their biggest threats, so go figure the two of them are gonna fight."

"How long 'til I can get outta here?" Selina wailed.

"They gave you some super dosage, so a few more hours at least. Before I turn in, I'll see if I can learn anything more about this tracker from my contacts. Tomorrow I'll get you and we'll get back on this together, alright?"

Chapter 5

A FTER A FITFUL NIGHT'S REST in the medical facility, Selina was released the next morning. Wexan met her at the front entrance, and they resumed their patrol. They both agreed the Tas Ralong markets were a decent place to try to find out if anything else like the Railen Tracker had showed up recently.

The markets at Tas Ralong filled a tremendous abandoned warehouse on the outskirts of town. Once a huge facility for fabricating structural pieces for buildings, and vehicles, the structure found new worth with its large open space where rows of vendors hawked their wares. From handy devices to weapons that were pretty useful if you had a need, the Trading Markets filled the bill from basic groceries to murder for hire and on the hush hush. Lots of the citizenry needed one or more of the above on any given day in Tas Ralong.

Selina clasped the tracker firmly in her hand, determined to not repeat her prior slip up. Wexan walked beside her. The Mardaks and others in their vicinity gave them a wide berth through the crowd. Sentry presence wasn't unheard of in the Markets, but it was definitely a wakeup call for everyone to hide any contraband they had recently decided to test on the black market. While contraband wasn't a known term in the markets, the people who lived nearby knew that just because you had it there didn't mean you kept it if a lawkeeper saw it.

The rows of vendor booths were topped with banners that billowed like weeds in an open field. "There," Wexan said as he pointed a few rows over to a red and black banner with a triangular logo in yellow on it.

"The Syndicates are bolder than I thought. They always hang their shingle over here like that?" Selina asked.

Wexan flipped a UA credit to a passing food vendor and swiped a roll for himself. As they walked and he gnawed at his snack, he commented with a semi full mouth. "Lots go on here that slips by the average enforcement groups. The Sentries and Militia have an understanding with the Syndicate and the Markets. They keep their dirty business between themselves, and we don't come in and bust all this up."

Selina eyed Wexan and shook her head. "I always thought we were here to shut people like that down."

"It's not always that simple, rookie. Sometimes, you need to get a little close to the people you're after, spend some time with 'em and learn how they think. It makes it easier to know what they're gonna do next, and even more important, where they're gonna do it."

Selina balled her free hand into a fist. While she knew Wexan had a point, something in her burned at just being around so much criminal activity. But then, they rounded a corner where she saw a group of Mardaks in tattered garments; they picked out semblances of clothing from large bins. A little further down the row a few Mardak traded items for hot stew.

Selina noticed Wexan had stopped as well and watched her. "See? Not that simple. This market's a lifeline for people since most of the industry left this world. Add Veculus to that, and you got a real problem. Look in these faces; if you can't see the fear there, you're plain blind. If we shut all this down like good little lawkeepers, how many won't have clothes to wear, how many kids won't have food?"

Hearing the plight of the average Zormad citizen really drove home to Selina how similar humans were to Mardaks after all. All of them lay claim to a decimated home world and a lifestyle where the primary concern was living to the next day, and what it took for surviving that. Selina swallowed hard and dabbed at her eye as they walked on. She activated her in set translator in a feeble attempt at distraction from the squalor around her. They soon ended up at the flag with the Syndicate logo, where an older Mardak woman sat at a table with several metallic objects at it.

"Hi, Kreela," Wexan said warmly.

Kreela nodded in kind to Wexan, but when she saw Selina and the tracker in her hand, she recoiled in her seat. "What's she doing with that?"

"Not using it, for sure." Selina narrowed her eyes.

"Kreela, this is my new partner, Selina Ravencraft. We found this yesterday during a firefight between Railen and Omegans by the old mineral processing district. We're wondering if there's any more of these around and what you know about anything the Railen or Omegans are doing."

Kreela grabbed for a curvy piece of metal. Selina thought at first she was going to use it to examine the tracker, but Kreela just wanted something to fiddle with in her fingers.

After a few moments, Kreela furrowed her brow and exhaled incredulously. "You got me. Syndicate's got a low presence here these days. But I know Network has been all open on the Looker hunt. Word is a knocked Looker'll get ya three million UA Credits, no questions asked. I suspect you'll see a lot more of these sooner or later."

Selina had heard about the process of Knocking. It was essentially a lock put on someone's cerebral capacities, turning them into a drone. Catching a Looker without incapacitating them was as useless as catching a fly on a piece of paper. The Railen Tracker incapacitated the Looker for a few minutes, but the process of Knocking locked their mind up and turned them into an obedient drone, where whoever had control of the Knocked person could command them as they wanted.

"So, they get them to locate Essence that way?" Selina asked.

"Well, Essence still ain't that easy to get. But without a Looker, you aren't even doing that much."

Kreela's lips formed a line and, her eyes locked in with Selina's. At first, Selina thought maybe Kreela had some kind of tick or palsy that made her stare; the Mardaks seemed to do that from time to time. Selina then remembered Grisha's gaze on her and how it ended up in a conversation starter. Finally, Kreela commented, "You seem very familiar to me."

"Oh? I'm sorry, I've never seen you before in my life."

"Maybe so. But there's a connection somewhere; I'm sensing it." She turned to the Railen Tracker and worked it over in her hands. Focused on it, she continued, "People go through life, through this Galaxy on this ball, and they think they rule their own existence. They think they control their own path, when in actuality we are connected. The past, the present, the future. People who raised us and are now gone away from this life, people we've yet to meet."

Selina's jaw twitched. Her defense mechanism toward anyone who attempted prying too deeply for her liking sprung like a well-made snare. "What are you talking about?"

"There's something about you, Selina Ravencraft. You're not telling me, maybe not even telling yourself, but you've got something in you that needs to be seen by everyone. Until you do that, you'll be always in a state of unrest."

Selina stepped back from the table. *Unrest? She has no idea. I wonder how much unrest she'd feel if her dad was slaughtered for standing his ground.* Tossing a look at Wexan, Selina stammered, "I'm feeling a little woozy; think I'll grab some food while you two finish up."

As she hurried off through the aisles, she glanced back and caught Wexan and Kreela as they chatted more about the tracker and probably Selina.

She arrived at a vendor who'd just served a crowd of Mardak and ordered a portion of Aquand, a concoction not far from Earth water. She plopped down at an empty table and sipped the slightly cool beverage. The partly sour, partly metallic taste tickled her tongue, but she was more interested in clearing her mind of what happened with Kreela.

Selina tried distracting her mind with their investigation, finding information on any Looker activity on Zormad and shutting it down when Kreela's words popped back into her head. *I've got something in me?* Selina thought. *Maybe she just meant my father and how he was killed. Of course I'm angry about that; who wouldn't be? That couldn't be it.*

Wexan found her twenty minutes later. "You keep bailing on me like this, I'm gonna ask for reassignment."

She finished the rest of her drink and swiped her mouth dry. "Sorry, Wexan, Kreela was a little hard to take."

Wexan gave a chuckle as Selina stood up. "Yeah, guess I should've warned you. Kreela's into UA Mysticism. Claims she's got the sight."

Selina nodded, her eyes astray from Wexan's. "Mmmhmmm."

Wexan shrugged. "Ehh, I never had much time for religion, me, but I know some swear by it. Like it's gonna resolve our issues one day. If that were the case, can't imagine all these people would be so hard up for Essence."

"I've no clue what she was getting at. I'd rather we get back to catching some criminals."

"Funny you say that. As I came over to find you, I got a notice on my comm unit. Energy theft in town. Perps just fled few minutes ago. Feel like a little fox hunt?"

Chapter 6

SELINA AND WEXAN CORNERED THE PERPS on the Energy theft and saved a huge relay system from being knocked offline. They returned the pieces back to the Mardaks, who restored the fragile but lingering power grid in Tas Ralong to its current state, mediocre as it was. Her shift ended, Selina headed back to NewEarth for a two-day break.

The Commissary was a common meeting ground on NewEarth. The facility was built in the hope it gave NewEarth citizens the beginning of a routine for their day, even if it was just a regular place where they congregated, satisfied their hunger, and even percolated the smallest bits of gossip on their neighbors. The traditions of gathering from Earth were carried over.

The Commissary was run by Ward Dixon, a former maintenance worker who'd helped with the establishment of NewEarth and had decided to kindle that one portion of the human existence, the sharing of stories and times good and not so good over whatever meager rations were available.

Ward's Commissary was a business, but since UA Credits weren't quite that common around NewEarth yet, Ward happily adopted a more or less barter type system, trading basic items, or even the occasional credit type transaction—whatever it took so people's bellies were full and the NewEarth community kept growing.

Ward greeted Selina as she came through the food line. His large belly pressed close to the counter as he scraped food portions onto Selina's tray. "How's my girl doing?" Ward said in his inimitable booming voice.

"Eh, surviving. Just finished my first shift with a Mardak."

"Oh boy, sorry to hear that."

"Right?" Selina chuckled.

Ward nodded sympathetically. "They come this way now and then; seen 'em when we do crop transfers. Bunch a smelly bastards."

"Try riding in a hover with one." Selina smiled.

Ward laughed. "'Suppose we gotta play nice though. Keeping order takes all the help we can get. I'm still seeing some theft around these parts too, ya know. Don't understand how people are so bent on taking things from their fellow humans."

"We all want more, especially when we've got so little."

"Yeah, I guess. So, how's your mama been? Ain't seen her too much." Ward's lips drew in a line.

Selina's eyes cast down a bit. "Recovering. I've been trying to slip her some extra water rations when I can. Dehydration sickness isn't pretty."

"No, it ain't. Tell ya what, I got some extras from my food prep. See me on your way out; I'll give you some."

"Aw, Ward, that's for your business."

"My business is taking care of people. If we don't look out for each other, who else will?" Ward extended a knobby hand to Selina.

She swallowed a lump in her throat and blinked hard to bat away a tear that formed. She hoped the waver in her voice wasn't noticed. "Thanks, Ward."

Selina grabbed her tray and made her way to a spot on the far end of the large hall. She felt better with her back against a windowless wall. Ever since Regulation training, Selina was told to be ever vigilant, as even in a small community like NewEarth, lawkeepers inevitably became targets of those who skirted the law. Selina enjoyed her meal in peace as the wafts of conversations drifted around her. She mustered her courage; her next visit wasn't going to be an easy one.

Chapter 7

SELINA HAD MIXED EMOTIONS AT VISITING her mother, and she hated the way she felt about it. Her mother still lived in the same place where Selina had grown up. It wasn't so much the childhood memories that made it difficult; it was being where her father no longer lived that made the domicile a repository of grief and loss. Selina wished like anything that the memory of her father wasn't so closely linked with the place, but she knew that wasn't an option. This home was and always would be the reminder of what her life had been and painfully now wasn't.

Selina's mother Laurina lay back on a makeshift couch, made of former insulation from the Ark Ship and reshaped into a contoured soft recliner. Her tired eyes greeted Selina as she entered. "Hello, my love."

"Hi, Mom. How's the back?"

Laurina grimaced as if her back answered Selina's question on cue. After a few attempts at shifting, she gave a deep sigh. "Been better. How was your shift?"

"Eventful. Got hit with a Railen Tracker and knocked out for a few hours."

Laurina's eyes darkened with worry. "Are you OK?"

"Mmmhmmm. They put me up in the Mardak medical wing. I finished my shift, and I'm headed back there in another day. I've been assigned to a filthy Mardak for a partner. They think I need more training, I guess."

Laurina squinted. "They aren't pushing you too much, are they?"

"It's OK, Mom, I can handle it." Selina knew, even if she'd just uttered a big lie, it was the only proper answer her mom needed for that question. Selina assumed her mother's concern was in part out of a sense of guilt or maybe responsibility to her dead husband that their only child was taken care of, even after that child became a grown woman with every right and ability at self-reliance.

Selina glanced around the room and saw the monitor against the wall broadcasting a feed of activity on Zormad, reports from the Trading Markets, alerts on raids from groups like the Railen and Omegans, as well as a link to Network, the combined signal of open comm transmissions and warrants throughout Ling Galaxy.

"They're finding more Lookers around here. Some in Tas Ralong, but my boss at the Regulation thinks NewEarth could be hit again soon," Selina muttered.

"There's nothing here they'd want." Laurina managed a laugh that quickly turned into heaves.

Selina fixed a portion of water for her mother. At her bedside, she cradled her mother's frail body as she took sips of the liquid. "Ward says hello, by the way."

Laurina smiled at the name. "Oh, that sweetie. Gotta get out and see him sometime, I do."

Selina knew, much as she denied it to others and even herself, the days for her mother weren't long. Dehydration sickness had already killed a number of NewEarth residents, and though Veculus hadn't worked its way into the human population, their odds in Ling Galaxy weren't that much different from the one they left behind.

Selina pushed back at the thoughts of death and worry about the future. It had been her routine since her teen years. Her father being gone left her to look out for her mother. She regretted the move to her own place, but she also craved the independence. However, as much as the oxygen in her lungs, Selina always made time and room for her mother, in spite of the awkwardness she felt over the visits.

Having her fill of the water ration, Laurina slumped back down. "Listen, before you go," she said weakly, "there's something you need to have. It's from your father. I'd tried to figure out a good time to give it to you, but there never seemed to be one, and then you were away at Regulation training."

Laurina pushed herself up to a sitting position amid a series of groans. She pointed to the far corner of the room, where a collection of boxes leaned against the wall in a haphazard pillar. "It's in one of those. Your father wanted you to have this when you were old enough. I never felt like it was the right time. In spite of the fact I still see you as my little girl, I know you're out making your way, and I'd much rather you get this than some raider if it ever came to that."

Selina grabbed the first box. It wobbled a bit, and her hands ran over the warped heavy cardboard texture, damaged by water and just the general decay of twenty years. The boxes contained a lot of items that weren't useful anymore: manuals and some basic electronics brought to Zormad in the hopes their components served some use, even if just a simple bartering for spare or better parts.

The second box held a collection of cold weather gear. Zormad did have a brutal winter, so the heavy cloaks weren't completely useless, but Laurina's gaze told Selina she hadn't found the item yet.

When the third box was uncovered, Selina knew she found it. She still had no idea what it was, but the sight of it alone told her; she even sensed something that told her she'd found it. A dark steel box, she held it up for Laurina to see. Laurina smiled a slightly sad grin, her eyes closed in a trance of memory. "Bring it here."

Selina piled the boxes back neat and rejoined her mother at bedside, the strange box on her lap. Selina felt the coolness of the steel, even through the fabric of her pants. Laurina slid her hands over Selina's and their eyes met. "You know, your father was one of the very first from Earth to set foot on this system. We made contact with Zormad before we landed, but they weren't interested in us just arriving here. Your father made the deal with the Mardaks that allowed us to land. There's still a lot of people who credit him with saving us. If we hadn't landed on Zormad, there's no telling how much further our life support systems would've taken us."

Laurina slid her hand along the sides of the box, and at once the box responded with a series of electronic chirps and a glowing blue emblem appeared.

"Not long after we arrived, Zormad fell under a raid from the Railen. I was pregnant with you at the time. The Railen had come looking for supplies, energy tech, who really knows? The Mardaks warned us that the Railen made runs on Zormad from time to time. I suspect Railen saw our little group as an easy mark, strays from another world who even the Mardaks weren't too concerned with. Maybe the Mardaks figured it was better that we got hit instead for a change.

"Your father had formed the first unit of what later became the Regulation. Anyhow, they had weapons from Earth. We'd brought enough with us for protection. We weren't the scared victims the Railen thought we were; not that first time, anyway. Humans fought the Railen off, and even managed to kill a few of them. They underestimated us and came with way less than they should have that first time.

"This was taken from the Railen by your father; he removed it from the dead hands of one of the raiders. We later found out it was a grave insult to the Railen, taking this from them. Regardless, your father knew, like the rest of NewEarth did, unless humans made a stand and let it be known we weren't here to be picked off like lambs at a slaughter, we'd never survive anywhere."

With that, Laurina moved her hand in a clockwise motion over the now humming box and the lid rotated in a like manner, eventually opening and showing a glowing bluish cylinder.

Laurina took a shuddered breath. Her eyes winced along with her voice, tinted with emotion. "I wish I could tell you more about this thing, but your father never had a chance to find out. Several days later, a bigger group of Railen appeared and targeted him while he was out with a group on an exploration of the further reaches of Zormad."

Selina started to reach for the device, but paused for a moment, remembering a little too well what grabbing a strange object did to her the last time. "Does anyone else know about this, Mom?"

"Well, Zed was closest to your father, and I know the two of them talked a lot about things like this. Check with him; maybe he can help you."

Zed was alongside Erick during the formation of the Regulation and was there that fateful day when the Regulation faced down the Railen threat. Since then, Zed assumed leadership of the Regulation.

Laurina's eyes were filled with wonder and a bit of sadness. She gazed at Selina though tears that lazily fell down her face. "I wish your father were here to see you now—our little girl all grown up and in charge of the world."

"I'm a shift worker, Mom. So far I've been in charge of getting myself assigned to a Mardak on a constant basis."

Laurina batted her eyes and swiped a tear away. "You're a fighter, like your father. You're stronger than you know, and one day you'll realize just who you're supposed to be."

Selina glanced downward. "Can you give me a hint?"

"Only you can know that, once you find the answer. But if you really want my opinion, it doesn't matter what happens; you'll always be our little Selina."

Selina swallowed the lump in her throat. Laurina's words were equal parts heartwarming and also more than a little wistful. "I'll be back sooner next time, Mom."

"Will you?"

Selina coughed and did her best to strain the emotion from her response. "Of course."

Chapter 8

THE DAY AFTER, SELINA BEGAN A NEW shift with Wexan. She kept the strange cylinder with her in case anyone, Railen or otherwise, came sniffing around for it. She slid the item into one of the inner pouches of her uniform. Before she began another day with Wexan, where they were scheduled for a pass through NewEarth, she knew she needed an answer about the device that cost her father's life.

This mysterious object from her father's past had grown from random curiosity to major mystery in her head. Selina wasn't putting it out of her mind anytime soon, and all the better to ask one of her own than chance any strange reaction from Wexan.

Like most areas in the precinct and NewEarth in general, Zed's office was a haphazard collection of equipment and hastily thrown together pieces of wall section cobbled from the Ark Ship remnants. A crude desk dominated the tiny office, a rare luxury only given to the upper tier of the Regulation.

Zed gazed at Selina's object on his desk. His palms were flat on either side of the cylinder. He eyed the item as if it were a holy relic and he feared his unclean spirit might combust if he touched it. "All this time, I thought he'd ditched it."

"Mom said you were there when he got it from the Railen."

Zed looked at Selina, but then his gaze rocketed past her into another realm. After a deep breath, he began, "We'd been on Zormad, I dunno, a week, maybe two? The Mardaks warned us about the Railen raids; said they came for anything good. It wasn't so much the Railen needed anything, they wanted to make sure everyone else had less.

"Erick knew as well as I and the rest that do or die, we had to hold up against them. We had a supply of weapons from Earth, of course, and so it happened; they sent a squad of Railen. I guess they'd sized us up and figured a colony of refugees wasn't worth much at all. But the Railen are scavengers, see? And, even the least threats have something of value, at least in the Railen mind. They walked into NewEarth, all high and mighty. By then we had a Network of tents while more permanent residences were being built. We did have the Ark Ship, which I'm sure was their initial target. We weren't as spread out yet, so it made the Railen easy to notice when they came calling."

As Zed continued with his story, Selina noticed his eyes lit up a bit. While the end was tragic for Selina's dad, she knew there was still a bit of pride, probably even felt by her father, over the stand that some lowly humans made in a strange

Galaxy against an alien race that could've well decimated NewEarth, for all they knew at the time.

Zed continued, "I met them first, but it wasn't long before the rest of the soldiers came front and center. The Railen at the front was dressed a little nicer than the rest. I approached, and he asked if I was the leader. You have to realize, at that point we were all alone here. The Mardaks had given us just enough space where we had a place to land and figure out what the hell we were gonna do.

"The Railen didn't waste a lot of time; they started blowing up parts of the Ark Ship. We'd barely started unloading the thing yet. Erick saw to it we had a sentry system in place, and that was about the only thing that saved us from being wiped out. Our troops were never all in one place; they all powered up and put fire on the Railen quick."

It was interesting to Selina hearing Zed's description of how spartan the early version of the Regulation was. By the time Selina joined the force, their methods and tactics had been refined into a sub military operation.

Zed continued, "People scattered, tried for any cover they could find, but there wasn't much. The Railen weapon fire was everywhere. I'd gotten turned around but fired shots back when I wasn't looking after wounded close to me.

"And then there was Erick, your dad. He laid down fire on the Railen like the rest of our group did, and pretty soon that little group of Railen was all but dusted. After the fight, we approached them, their bodies just flung to the ground. One of them was still clinging to life, and he had this thing in his hands. He just lay there, wounded, bleeding out bluish green blood all over the place. He eyed Erick and me hard. I'll always remember that look in the Railen's eyes; I can't imagine what happened that gave him that level of hate, and especially to us, who'd just appeared on Zormad a few days earlier. He started to reach for another pistol to shoot when Erick stopped him, his rifle beaded on his head. Erick told him to stand down, but either he ignored him, or more likely, didn't understand English. Anyhow, he'd attacked us, and we figured there wasn't a solution that included a peaceful discussion, so Erick sent him to the great beyond.

"Anyway, whatever the Railen said was lost on us, but Erick kept the thing. He figured if it was that valuable to the Railen, it may come in handy, especially on the markets."

"Had you ever asked around? Maybe the Mardaks know what it is?"

"We showed it to a few Mardak Sentries, but aside from wanting nothing to do with it, a few more knowledgeable folks said it's a disruptor. It deactivates weapons in the near vicinity, but no one's said anything else."

Zed slid the disruptor carefully back toward Selina. "Given who Erick was and what he did for us all, I never felt right keeping this. If it's anyone's, it's yours. I'd keep it outta sight, especially from your Mardak partner over there."

Selina nodded. She returned the disruptor to its hiding place on her uniform. "Well, that's more than I knew before. Thanks, Zed."

Zed smiled in reply. "Your dad and I always looked out for each other. After he died, I tried to make sure you were OK. I gotta admit I wasn't crazy about you joining the Regulation. I had half a mind to reject your application. But we need all the help we can get. Besides, once I heard you ripped it up in training, dusting your classmates, I knew you had your daddy's spirit and you belonged here."

Selina swelled at the mention of her father, but also bristled a little at the comparison. She knew there was no changing her
origin, but she hoped Zed and everyone else realized she had her own destiny and that it wasn't necessarily Erick's.

Selina rejoined Wexan in the NewEarth region for another leg of their shift. Her uniform had gotten a little tighter, as she included the Railen Tracker with the disruptor in another hidden location. Wexan decided he wasn't ready for handing it over, since the situation on Zormad after their run in with the Railen and Omegan brawl hadn't settled one bit.

Selina took the controls of their vehicle and guided them through the regions of the colony. As their time on Zormad continued into a third decade, humans learned more about Zormad and what kind of materials were available, which brought with it a change in the look of the living quarters. NewEarth housing soon took on a semblance of places like Tas Ralong, minus the towering facilities.

This wasn't lost on Wexan, who marveled at how Xeno scum managed to blend in with the Zormad architecture, if only slightly. "Never thought I'd see a bunch of filthy Xeno making their way here. I gave your kind a month, and look at you now," Wexan said.

"Don't count us out." Selina chuckled. "Hey, how did our last energy thieves do?"

"Oh, them? Mardak Council took care of them but good. They threw them in for some hard labor for three years, trying to make an example of 'em."

"Wow, didn't think Mardaks ever got that hard on crime."

"Things are changing, rookie. Got a new magistrate running things now, and they mean business."

Selina smiled. Zormad had full opportunity to slide into destruction and chaos, but since humans now called it home, that was never acceptable for Selina. At least, not until humans figured out their next move in their new Galaxy. She turned their vehicle up a straightaway alongside the gigantic hulk of the Ark Ship.

Chapter 9

SELINA'S MIND HAD JUST ABOUT SETTLED into the humdrum of the ordinary when the vehicle comm disrupted their routine moment. "Units in immediate vicinity of Region Alpha respond. Repeat: units respond to Region Alpha; group of Railen spotted approaching."

Selina swallowed hard as she gunned the engine. Wexan said, "Could be a group of trollers, looking for useful trash."

"Inside NewEarth boundaries? I don't think so." Selina shot Wexan a worried glance. A dreadful feeling slid over her as their vehicle hurtled toward Region Alpha. She thought back to Zed's story, and wondered if the Railen were back for the disruptor this time. NewEarth wasn't a hot bed of production, and what they had back from the previous Railen raid hadn't improved much since—things were just more dust covered and worn out than before.

After rounding their vehicle around the broad side of the Ark Ship, they spotted the Railen group when they were still a half mile from Region Alpha. It was hard to miss; the Railen craft's huge wings rose a few hundred feet in the air. This collection of Railen was bigger than the one from Zed's story; the onboard computer identified a group of at least thirty, all heavily armed.

"This is an invasion," Wexan muttered. "I'm notifying Mardak Militia. We can't stop 'em here, and Tas Ralong's too close. I gotta call this in to my base."

Selina gunned the accelerator until they arrived where the Regulation troops had gathered in a defensive position across from the Railen. She pulled over alongside a grouping of Regulation vehicles. So far the Railen had just moved troops up but hadn't attacked yet.

Selina saw Jared making a report on the comm and headed over to him. "They hadn't said what they wanted, but they're standing in place. It's like they were ordered here by someone."

Selina felt the disruptor in its secret hiding place as it grew warm. And as if in sequence, she saw a group of Railen, with some kind of monitoring device ahead of them, yell and shout, pointing in her direction.

"That can't be good," Selina muttered.

One Railen stepped toward the gathered Regulation forces. He tapped a control on his suit, and his helmet vanished quickly into nothing. Selina gazed deep into the Railen's gray eyes, and she really got the irony of calling any one feature on a Railen gray when their entire physical form was a study in the shade.

"My name is Darrick Bruer, and we want what your kind took from us."

Jared cleared his throat. "You've got some nerve. The Railen steal whatever they want, from NewEarth and elsewhere."

Darrick's gaze shot to Jared; his eyes smoldered in response. Then he said, "Xeno scum, one day you'll all learn your place here, and it's not for you to decide what I need to explain."

"Start over, Railen trash." Jared shook his head.

Darrick took a steadied breath. His fingers gnashed together as his hands formed fists. Whoever this guy was, Selina thought, he sure wasn't a chief diplomat.

"It's very simple. One of your kind has a disruptor and it doesn't belong with you. We're here to take it back, even if we have to level your little settlement here to do it."

"Stand down and we'll talk." Jared's reply came through his gnashed teeth.

"Xeno, hear me well." Darrick pointed a finger to Selina. "We've confirmed a signature on her of the device we want. Give it, or her, to us, and we'll leave without further trouble."

Jared glanced slightly to Selina but quickly eyed Darrick again. "We don't negotiate with hostiles."

Selina felt her gut tense. She slid one hand over the disruptor's location on her suit, still hidden from plain sight. She'd never seen it in action, and wasn't about to pull a quick draw. The other Railen behind Darrick drew their weapons and, in a coordinated series of howls, trained them on Selina. The collective whine of activate pulse rifles filled the air, in a chorus of danger.

"Xeno, you really think we're the kind that looks the other way or just forgets a slight like theft? Your time in Ling Galaxy is sure to be full of painful lessons, I foresee."

Wexan grabbed for Selina and shoved her behind him. "This ain't a firing squad. Zormad's got a system, at least part of one. Only way we'll ever get peace here is through order. We aren't letting anyone blast someone else away just 'cause they suspect something."

But Wexan's words fell on deaf ears. The Railen to a one, opened fire on the gathered troops. The Regulation forces crouched and returned the shots. The air exploded in a sea of blasts from the Railen front with return fire from the Regulation. Selina rolled and returned fire herself; her shots landed a few glancing blows on the Railen.

Selina heard Jared yell and saw him fall to the ground. She scampered to his side, but he waved her back. He shouted commands to her and the rest of the Regulation in earshot as a thick ooze of blood trailed from his lips.

Wexan yelled over his shoulder to Selina. "Back to the hover, and get outta here! Mardak Militia's en route; I just hope they make it before it's too late!"

Selina and Wexan made a beeline for their vehicle as the rest of the Railen party advanced and fired at random at the gathered force of Regulation troops.

Selina and Wexan were almost to the hover when the sound of Darrick's voice to their side stopped them in their tracks. There he stood, the reddish glow of his weapon staring Selina and Wexan down like an angry eye.

"Not another step. Hand it over."

Darrick's gaze locked in on Selina. She thought about the disruptor, how her dad and mom held it all those years, and how her father was killed by a Railen because of it. She knew in her gut whatever this device meant to Darrick, for her it meant her father's life. That wasn't something she threw away on a demand. However, the sight of Darrick's rifle trained on her had Selina worried she was about to pay the same price Erick had.

Selina searched Wexan's face for their next move. Wexan eyed Darrick, then Selina, and she saw a look in Wexan's eye she'd never seen before. This Mardak, who sworn earlier her life wasn't even worth the paperwork it took to explain it, jumped in between Selina and Darrick, his rifle raised, but before he got off a volley, Darrick emptied a barrage into Wexan's midsection, littering the area with grayish Mardak blood and innards.

Time froze a bit as Selina watched her partner crumble to the ground slowly. She gasped at the sight of Wexan, the first Mardak she'd ever really known at all. To say she knew Wexan was a stretch too, but in their hours together, they'd managed a sort of ease with each other. Theirs wasn't a warm association, but their grouping had a kind of teacher-student familiarity, and suddenly Selina wondered about his last gesture and how much Wexan's earlier disinterest toward her was a front.

From the look of it, she'd be able to ask Wexan in person in the afterlife shortly.

A thousand thoughts flooded her mind. Plans unmet, promises unfulfilled, a future unlived. Selina felt though, if her death was here, she was ready. The rest of her crew were too far away, still engaging the Railen, and they wouldn't have made it in time. She pulled in a deep breath and waited for her end.

A crackling sound erupted around her. Her entire body tensed, a flash of light engulfed her, and then darkness and void. She tried to feel for something, anything, but instead of a sense of peace, an excruciating headache came over her. And then, her eyes opened and she saw she was in a room, but her vision was too blurry to identify anything

A mechanical droning sound was a clue her surroundings had indeed changed. Furthermore, the way the room eased back and forth on occasion, made her suspect she'd somehow left Zormad altogether. She blinked her eyes, but the room was still too blurry and dark for making out anything.

Selina then noticed she lay on a mattress. It was moderately firm. She noticed a nearby pedestal with a digital readout display and thought, *Maybe it's some kind of sick bay area like the Mardak infirmary.*

A gruff male voice spoke. "Take it easy. You've been out for the past twenty minutes."

Selina looked around and saw an outline of a person, but her vision was still too fuzzy. "I had to grab you in a hurry; once I saw Darrick with a bead on you, I knew time was short."

Selina's eyes focused a bit more and saw the body that went with the voice. A pilot; from the looks of it. "My name's Ket Durban, but you can call me Ket. You're on my ship, the *Crimson Lance.*"

Selina rubbed her temples together until she realized it did absolutely no good at all. "What're you doing? You've gotta get me back to Zormad."

"Back to Zormad? Honey, you were in a big ass hot spot back there. If I hadn't grabbed you right then, you'd be a whiff of vapor right now."

Selina's throat tensed as she thought of her group, the Regulation, Wexan, Jared. They were under attack, and she'd left them. "You don't understand. They're my people, they're all I know, all I have. My mother—"

Ket looked on her with compassion. "I'm sorry, I would've stuck around longer, but me and the Railen go way back, and not in a good way."

"Uh huh."

Selina glanced about the room for anything she could've used to bludgeon Ket for a quick getaway. But nothing looked promising enough, and then he said, "So, what's your name?"

"Selina. Now that we're exchanging names, you mind telling me what the hell you were doing with a ship around Zormad and NewEarth?"

Ket's eyes widened. "Really? I save your ass from getting vaped, and you're questioning me? I don't know if Xeno have a saying like 'thank you', but that's a customary response when people in Ling Galaxy get favors like the one I just did you."

"You took me from a fight. My people were being slaughtered by the Railen."

"Uh huh, and you'd have been there with them, charred remains in that field." Ket's mouth formed in a line. "Look, that Clutch I yanked you here with can throw anyone for a loop. Just sit there a few minutes, get your head together, then I'll school you on gratitude."

Selina wriggled back in her seat, put off by Ket's cavalier attitude. She racked her brain over why she was taken, and not others. Could Ket have known about the disruptor? She sighed with relief when she felt it still safely in its hiding spot. Not only that, the Railen Tracker was still there too.

Selina lay back down. As Ket left the room, she activated her Digivisor. The reddish block over Ket's frame made her chuckle and wonder where gratitude ended and obligation began.

The Essence Wars Series

All of these titles are available individually on Amazon.com

Have you read the Valkyrie Chronicles Series?

Forced into a life she hates by the government of Lebabolis, the last human nation on Earth, Ana Crucinal must comply with her pre-ordained future or undergo Realignment. But when her brother falls ill, Ana joins up with the resistance in an attempt to flee Lebabolis—only to learn that the true threat lies elsewhere: an alien race known as the Omegans. All of this was foreseen. A thousand years ago a man living in New Orleans had imagined the future Ana now lives in. He wrote about the resistance, the alien menace, everything. Desperate to save themselves and the remnants of the human race, the resistance formulates a plan to do the only thing they can think of: travel back in time to save the future.

With her enemies closing in, Ana knows this is her one chance to save herself, her brother, and the resistance. Failure is death and the never-ending enslavement of humanity.

Buy the books of the Valkyrie Chronicles Series on Amazon today and find out why so many have fallen in love with Ana and her mission.

Want a free story?

Destination Exodus is a prequel story I wrote for the Essence Wars series you just read. This story features Erick Ravencraft, father of Selina Ravencraft, as part of the group of humans who leave Earth and the Milky Way galaxy in the hopes of survival. Can they navigate the dangers standing between them and their goal? Go to the following URL to get your free copy! www.paulheingarten.com/email-list/

The Essence Wars Continue!

Crucible of Legacy, the first FULL LENGTH novel in the Essence Wars Series, is coming soon! Get ready to hear the story of Pierce Sava, son of the current ruler of the Universal Alliance, Nic Sava. Pierce had more than a few disagreements on how things were run, and decided it best he went his own way, in the wilds of Ling Galaxy. Employed by the Syndicates, Pierce is content with his life of running cargoes and mixing it up with his friend Ket Durban. But, when the UA and Nic Sava face a crisis, can Pierce find it within himself to return to the life and the love he left behind, to help the UA restore their crumbling order as the Essence Wars rage on?

About the Author

Paul Heingarten spreads time between writing, being a musician, and, since 2002, a career in Information Technology. He lives in the southern United States with his wife Andrea.

Other Titles by Paul Heingarten

The Harvest (short story)
Leave from Absence (novel)
The Monitor (short story)
Natural Election (short story)
Cataclysm Epoch (novel)
Settling Darkness (novel)
Valkyrie Rising (novel)
Menace Ascending (short story)
Xeno Reckoning (novelette)
Gambit of Dares (novelette)
Quest for Dominion (novelette)
Quantum of Destiny (novelette)
Vengeance Directive (novelette)
Balance of Retribution (novelette)
Destination Exodus (short story)
Revenge Nexus (novelette)
Stratagem Awakening (novelette)
Collateral Crisis (novelette)